STAR WARS

EPISODE VI
RETURN OF THE JEDI

VOLUME TWO

Script
ARCHIE GOODWIN

Art
AL WILLIAMSON
CARLOS GARZÓN

Colors
CARY PORTER
PERRY McNAMEE

Lettering
ED KING

Cover Art
AL WILLIAMSON

DARK HORSE COMICS

Spotlight

VISIT US AT
www.abdopublishing.com

Reinforced library bound edition published in 2010 by Spotlight, a division of the ABDO Group, 8000 West 78th Street, Edina, Minnesota 55439. Spotlight produces high-quality reinforced library bound editions for schools and libraries. Published by agreement with Dark Horse Comics, Inc., and Lucasfilm Ltd.

Printed in the United States of America, Melrose Park, Illinois.
092009
012010

 PRINTED ON RECYCLED PAPER

Library of Congress Cataloging-in-Publication Data

Goodwin, Archie.
  Episode VI : return of the Jedi / based on the screenplay by George Lucas ; script adaptation Archie Goodwin ; artists Al Williamson & Carlos Garzon ; letterer Ed King. -- Reinforced library bound ed.
     p. cm. -- (Star wars)
  "Dark Horse Comics."
  ISBN 978-1-59961-705-3 (vol. 1) -- ISBN 978-1-59961-706-0 (vol. 2) -- ISBN 978-1-59961-707-7 (vol. 3) -- ISBN 978-1-59961-708-4 (vol. 4)
  1. Graphic novels. [1. Graphic novels.] I. Lucas, George, 1944- II. Williamson, Al, 1931- III. Garzon, Carlos. IV. Return of the Jedi (Motion picture) V. Title. VI. Title: Episode six. VII. Title: Return of the Jedi.
  PZ7.7.G656Epk 2010
  [Fic]--dc22
                                      2009030862

All Spotlight books have reinforced library bindings and are manufactured in the United States of America.

Episode VI

RETURN OF THE JEDI™

Volume 2

While the Emperor begins construction on the second Death Star—a space station more powerful than the first—the Rebellion prepares for their next move against the Empire.

Rebel leader Princess Leia and Jedi Luke Skywalker have traveled to Tatooine to rescue Han Solo from gangster Jabba the Hutt.

But their mission has not gone as planned; Leia has been enslaved, and Luke captured, by Jabba. Now, above a pit in the Dune Sea, Luke and Han are about to be fed to a fearsome Sarlacc!

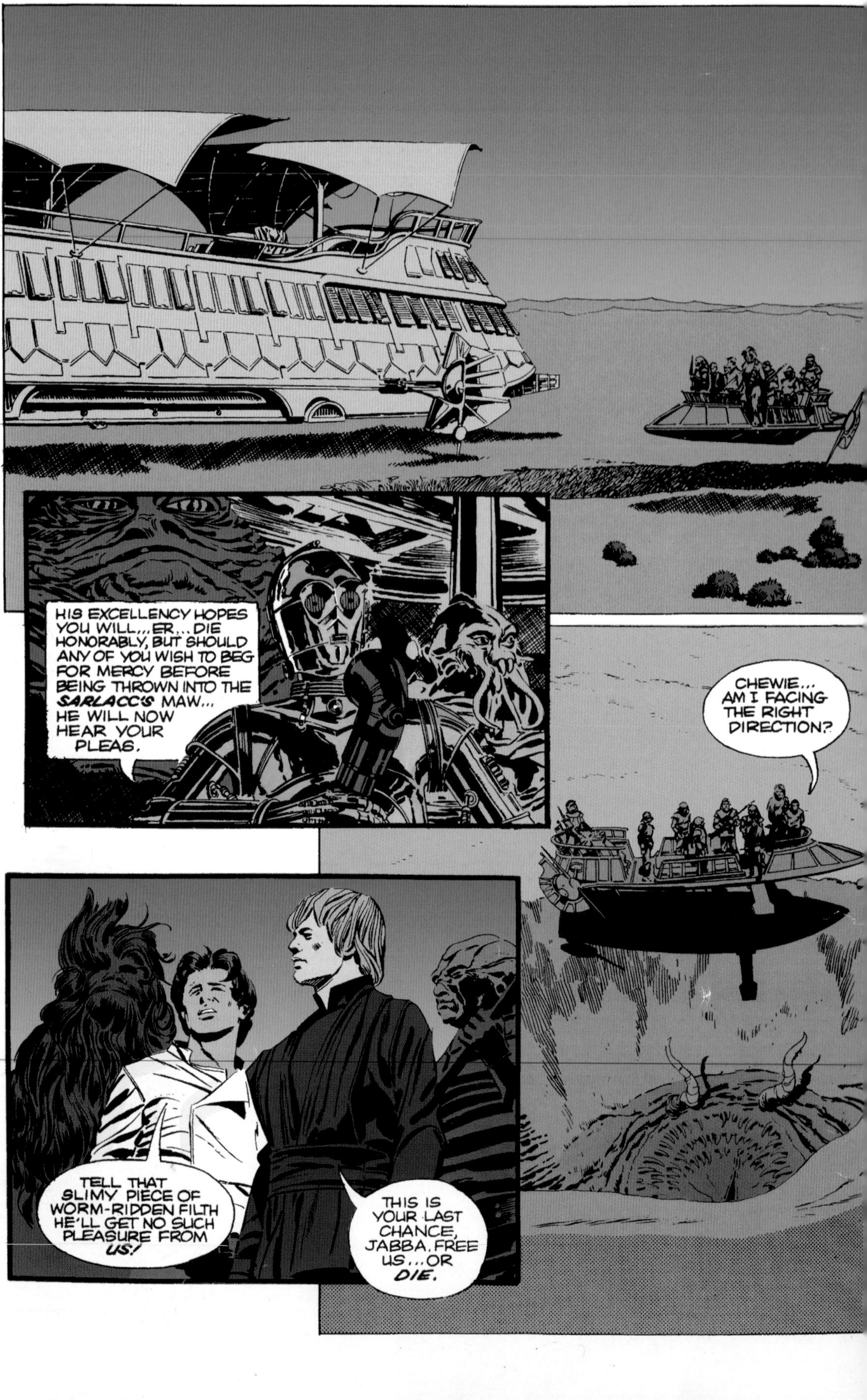
HIS EXCELLENCY HOPES YOU WILL... ER... DIE HONORABLY, BUT SHOULD ANY OF YOU WISH TO BEG FOR MERCY BEFORE BEING THROWN INTO THE *SARLACC'S* MAW... HE WILL NOW HEAR YOUR PLEAS.
CHEWIE... AM I FACING THE RIGHT DIRECTION?
TELL THAT SLIMY PIECE OF WORM-RIDDEN FILTH HE'LL GET NO SUCH PLEASURE FROM *US!*
THIS IS YOUR LAST CHANCE, JABBA. FREE US... OR *DIE.*

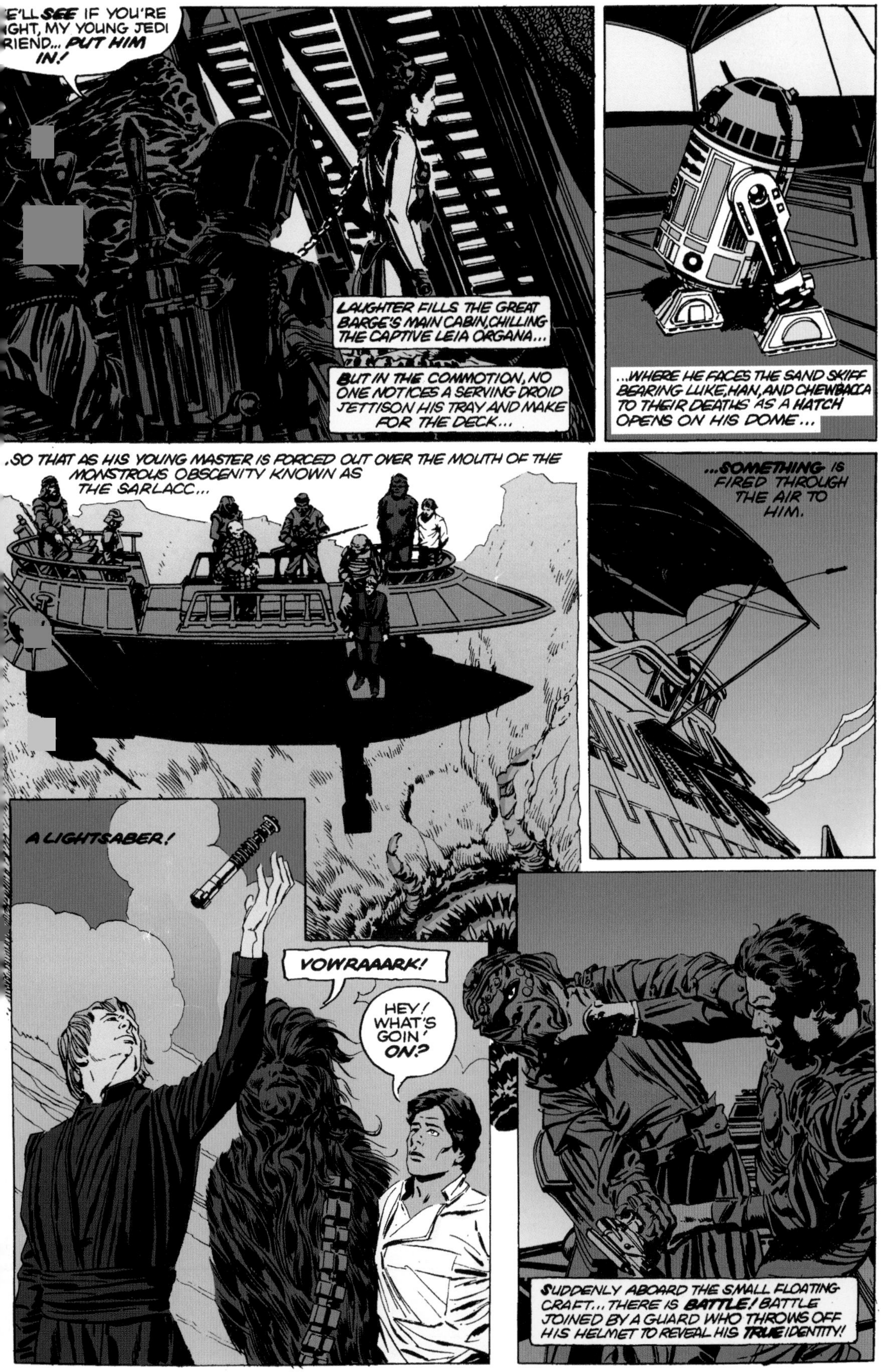

E'LL SEE IF YOU'RE IGHT, MY YOUNG JEDI RIEND... PUT HIM IN!
LAUGHTER FILLS THE GREAT BARGE'S MAIN CABIN, CHILLING THE CAPTIVE LEIA ORGANA...
BUT IN THE COMMOTION, NO ONE NOTICES A SERVING DROID JETTISON HIS TRAY AND MAKE FOR THE DECK...
...WHERE HE FACES THE SAND SKIFF BEARING LUKE, HAN, AND CHEWBACCA TO THEIR DEATHS AS A HATCH OPENS ON HIS DOME...
.SO THAT AS HIS YOUNG MASTER IS FORCED OUT OVER THE MOUTH OF THE MONSTROUS OBSCENITY KNOWN AS THE SARLACC...
...SOMETHING IS FIRED THROUGH THE AIR TO HIM.
A LIGHTSABER!
VOWRAAARK!
HEY! WHAT'S GOIN' ON?
SUDDENLY ABOARD THE SMALL FLOATING CRAFT... THERE IS BATTLE! BATTLE JOINED BY A GUARD WHO THROWS OFF HIS HELMET TO REVEAL HIS TRUE IDENTITY!

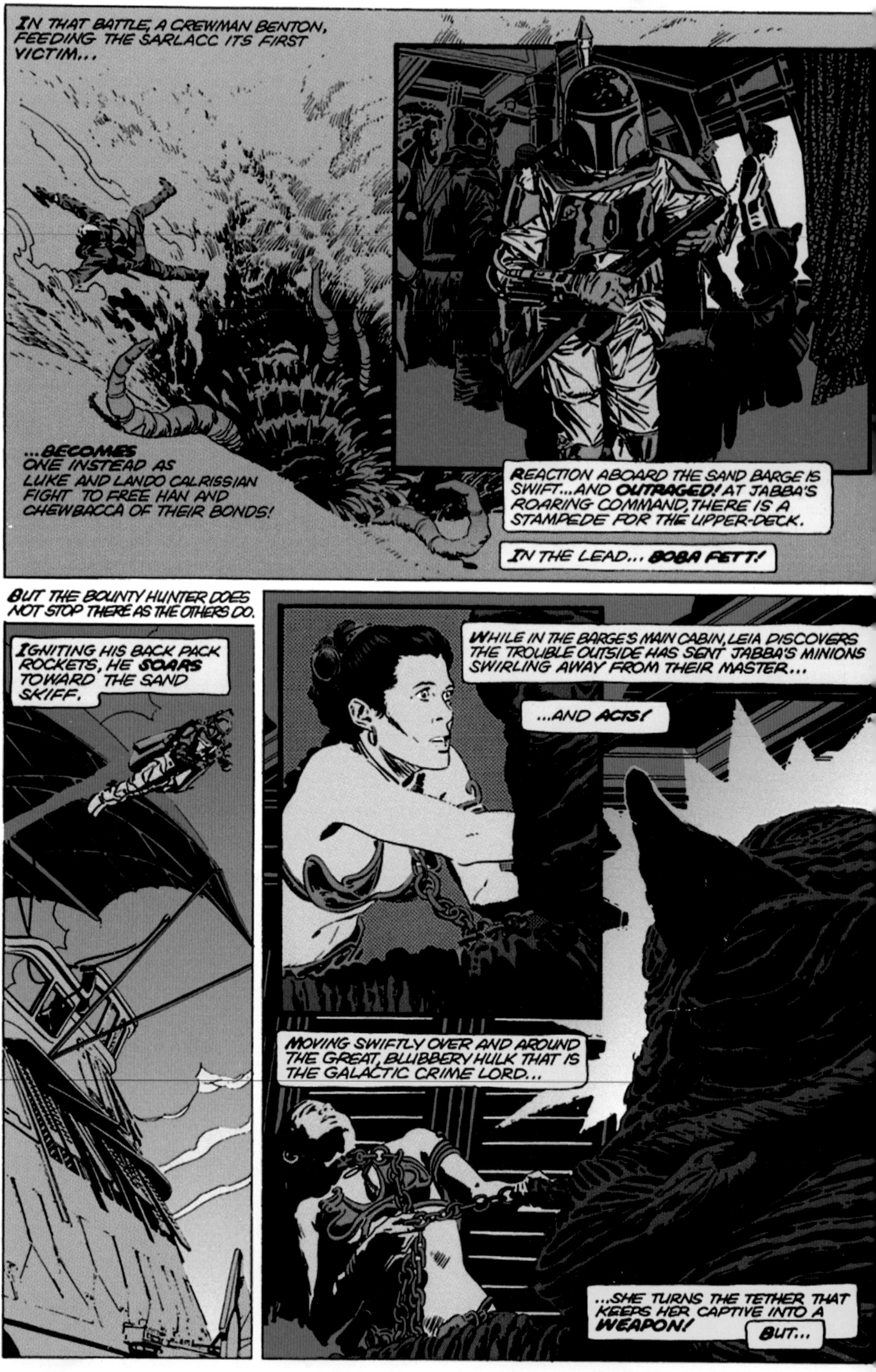
IN THAT BATTLE, A CREWMAN BENTON, FEEDING THE SARLACC ITS FIRST VICTIM...
...BECOMES ONE INSTEAD AS LUKE AND LANDO CALRISSIAN FIGHT TO FREE HAN AND CHEWBACCA OF THEIR BONDS!
REACTION ABOARD THE SAND BARGE IS SWIFT...AND OUTRAGED! AT JABBA'S ROARING COMMAND, THERE IS A STAMPEDE FOR THE UPPER-DECK.
IN THE LEAD... BOBA FETT!
BUT THE BOUNTY HUNTER DOES NOT STOP THERE AS THE OTHERS DO.
IGNITING HIS BACK PACK ROCKETS, HE SOARS TOWARD THE SAND SKIFF.
WHILE IN THE BARGE'S MAIN CABIN, LEIA DISCOVERS THE TROUBLE OUTSIDE HAS SENT JABBA'S MINIONS SWIRLING AWAY FROM THEIR MASTER...
...AND ACTS!
MOVING SWIFTLY OVER AND AROUND THE GREAT, BLUBBERY HULK THAT IS THE GALACTIC CRIME LORD...
...SHE TURNS THE TETHER THAT KEEPS HER CAPTIVE INTO A WEAPON!
BUT...

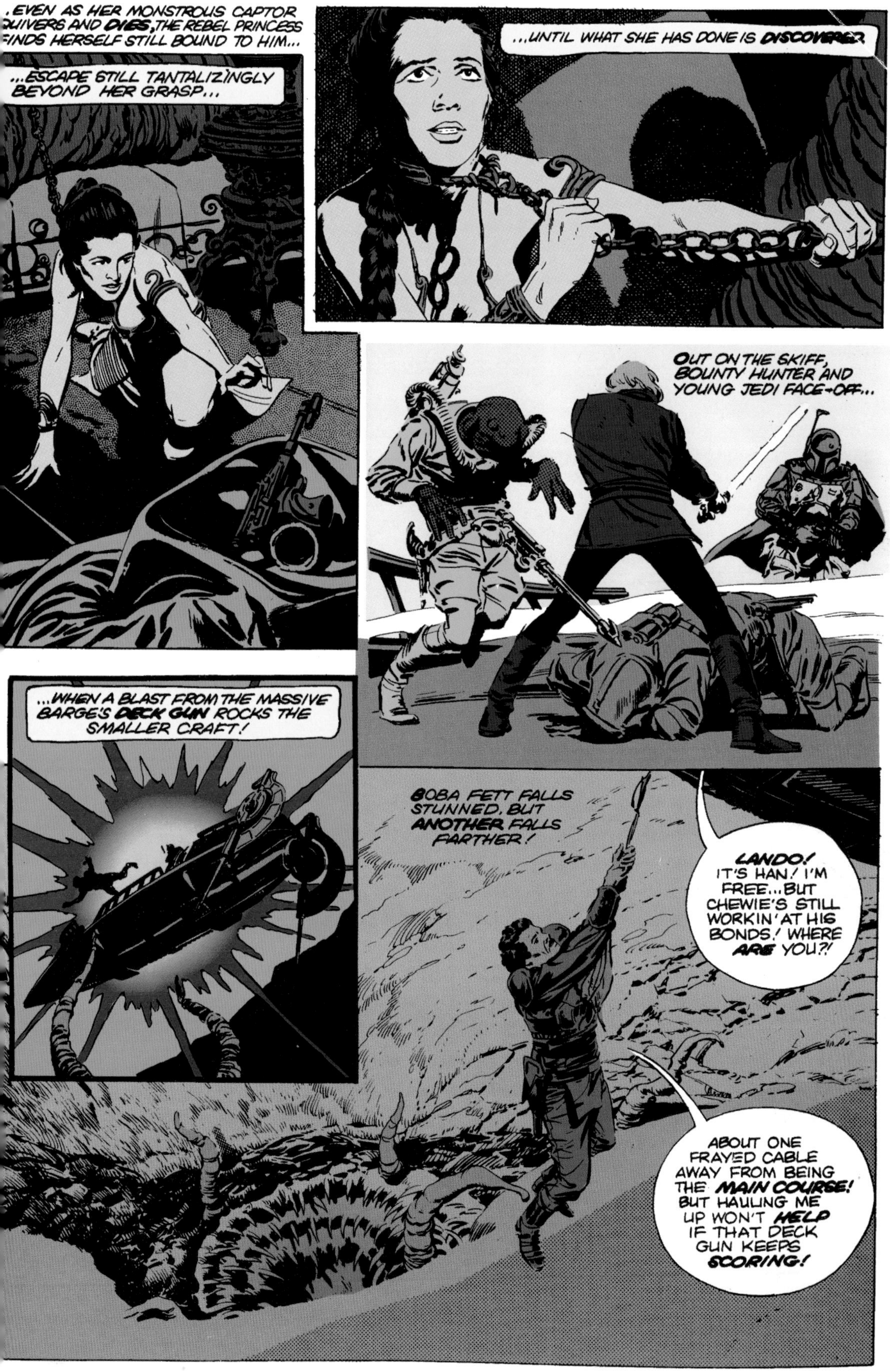
...EVEN AS HER MONSTROUS CAPTOR QUIVERS AND DIES, THE REBEL PRINCESS FINDS HERSELF STILL BOUND TO HIM...
...ESCAPE STILL TANTALIZINGLY BEYOND HER GRASP...
...UNTIL WHAT SHE HAS DONE IS DISCOVERED.
OUT ON THE SKIFF, BOUNTY HUNTER AND YOUNG JEDI FACE-OFF...
...WHEN A BLAST FROM THE MASSIVE BARGE'S DECK GUN ROCKS THE SMALLER CRAFT!
BOBA FETT FALLS STUNNED, BUT ANOTHER FALLS FARTHER!
LANDO! IT'S HAN! I'M FREE...BUT CHEWIE'S STILL WORKIN' AT HIS BONDS! WHERE ARE YOU?!
ABOUT ONE FRAYED CABLE AWAY FROM BEING THE MAIN COURSE! BUT HAULING ME UP WON'T HELP IF THAT DECK GUN KEEPS SCORING!

AS THE GAMBLER AND ORIGINAL OWNER OF THE **MILLENNIUM FALCON** SHOUTS, LUKE SKYWALKER IS ALREADY MOVING...

...AS THE DAMAGED SKIFF CAREENS MOMENTARILY CLOSER TO THE SAIL BARGE...

...LANDING HIGH, SOMERSAULTING FORWARD...

...TO LAND AMID ENRAGED AND DETERMINED ENEMIES!

ONE BY ONE, THEY **FALL** TO THE FLASHING LIGHTSABER! BUT **OTHERS** APPEAR TO TAKE THEIR PLACE...

...AND THE DECK GUN KEEPS **FIRING!**

LANDO...? ARE YOU **NEAR?** CAN YOU GRAB **THIS!**

IF THE **CABLE** HOLDS AND YOU DON'T POKE ME IN THE **EYE!** GET IT **CLOSER...!** TO MY **HAND!**

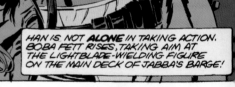

HAN IS NOT **ALONE** IN TAKING ACTION. BOBA FETT RISES, TAKING AIM AT THE LIGHTBLADE-WIELDING FIGURE ON THE MAIN DECK OF JABBA'S BARGE!

GROWL FROM CHEWBACCA ALERTS HAN! DESPERATELY, HE SWINGS THE SPEAR BEING EXTENDED TO LANDO! BUT...

YOU INTERFERING BLIND *GAWK!* YOU'RE *NEXT!*

IGNORING THE BLINDED CORELLIAN'S WILD ATTEMPTS TO STRIKE AGAIN, THE BOUNTY HUNTER RE-AIMS AT WHAT HE CONSIDERS TO BE HIS MOST *DANGEROUS* FOE...

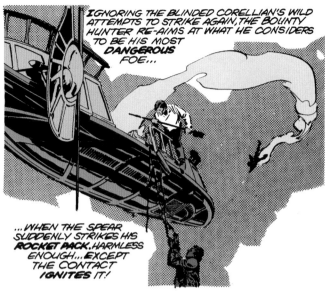

...WHEN THE SPEAR SUDDENLY STRIKES HIS *ROCKET PACK.* HARMLESS ENOUGH... *EXCEPT* THE CONTACT *IGNITES* IT!

THE MAN WHO SOLD HIS SERVICES TO BOTH DARTH VADER AND JABBA THE HUTT SOARS *HIGH*...

...AND FALLS *FAR,* TO THE SARLACC'S PLEASURE.

ROWRAAAARK!

I DID *THAT...?* WISH I COULD HAVE *SEEN* IT!

BUT ONLY *ONE* DANGER IS ELIMINATED... AS A BLAST FROM THE DECK GUN OF THE SAIL BARGE *REMINDS* THEM!

WHILE IN THE BARGE'S MAIN CABIN...

VREE-DITTA TUH-WHOOOOT!

ARTOO! THANK THE FORCE IT WAS *YOU* WHO FOUND ME! NOW LET'S GET *OUT* OF HERE!

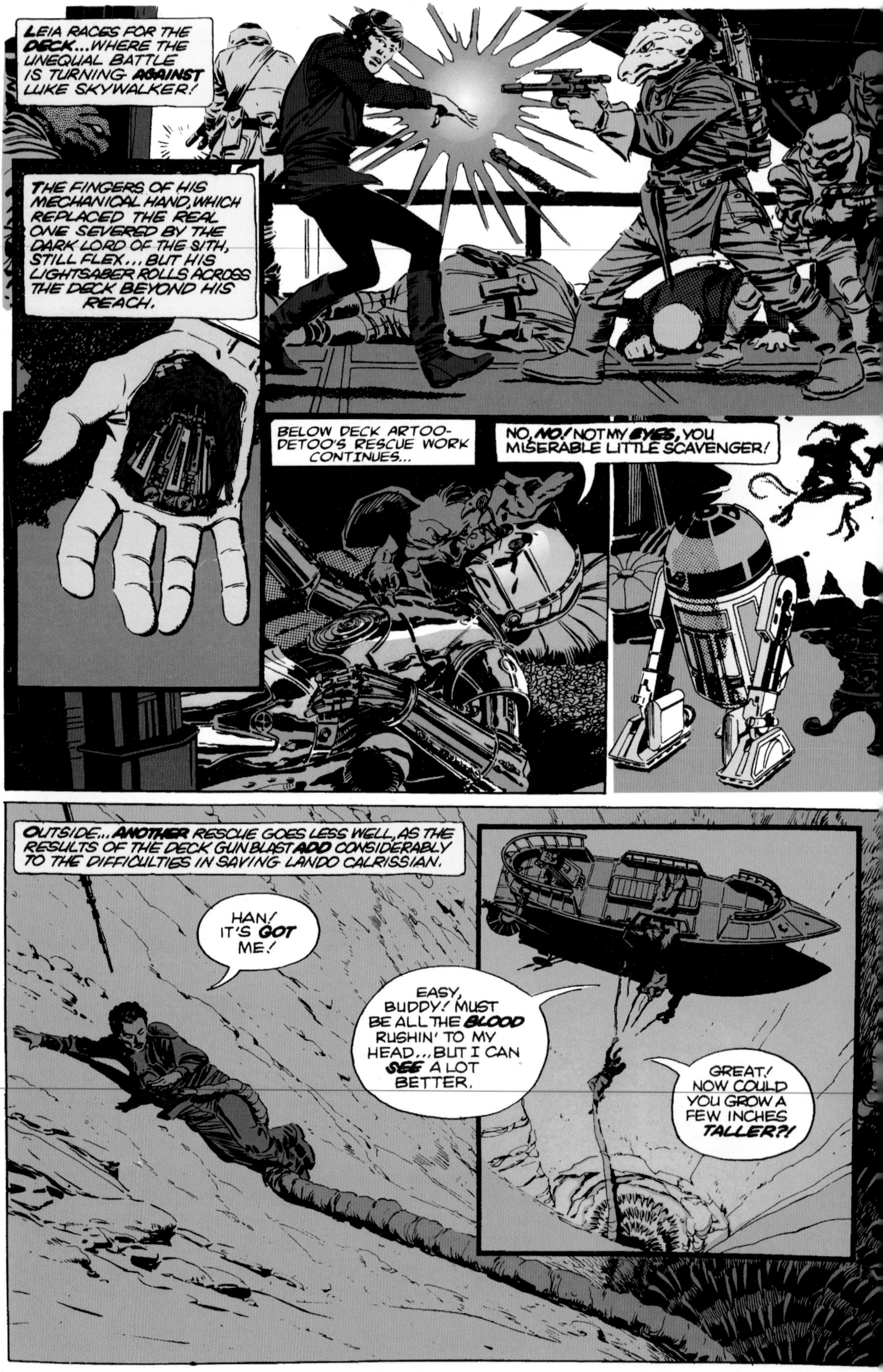

LEIA RACES FOR THE DECK... WHERE THE UNEQUAL BATTLE IS TURNING AGAINST LUKE SKYWALKER!
THE FINGERS OF HIS MECHANICAL HAND, WHICH REPLACED THE REAL ONE SEVERED BY THE DARK LORD OF THE SITH, STILL FLEX... BUT HIS LIGHTSABER ROLLS ACROSS THE DECK BEYOND HIS REACH.
BELOW DECK ARTOO-DETOO'S RESCUE WORK CONTINUES...
NO, NO! NOT MY EYES, YOU MISERABLE LITTLE SCAVENGER!
OUTSIDE... ANOTHER RESCUE GOES LESS WELL, AS THE RESULTS OF THE DECK GUN BLAST ADD CONSIDERABLY TO THE DIFFICULTIES IN SAVING LANDO CALRISSIAN.
HAN! IT'S GOT ME!
EASY, BUDDY! MUST BE ALL THE BLOOD RUSHIN' TO MY HEAD... BUT I CAN SEE A LOT BETTER.
GREAT! NOW COULD YOU GROW A FEW INCHES TALLER?!

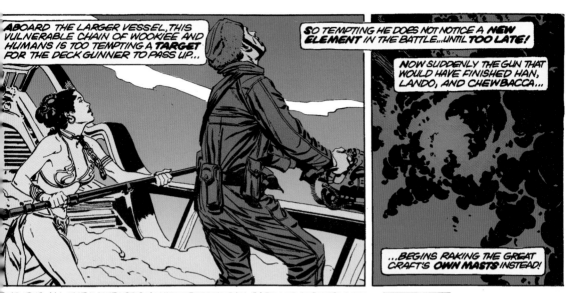

ABOARD THE LARGER VESSEL, THIS VULNERABLE CHAIN OF WOOKIEE AND HUMANS IS TOO TEMPTING A *TARGET* FOR THE DECK GUNNER TO PASS UP...

SO TEMPTING HE DOES NOT NOTICE A *NEW ELEMENT* IN THE BATTLE...UNTIL *TOO LATE!*

NOW SUDDENLY THE GUN THAT WOULD HAVE FINISHED HAN, LANDO, AND CHEWBACCA...

...BEGINS RAKING THE GREAT CRAFT'S *OWN MASTS* INSTEAD!

AND IT IS ALL THE DISTRACTION LUKE NEEDS TO CALL BACK HIS LIGHTBLADE.

AIM IT *DOWN,* LEIA! FIRE AT THE *DECK!* I'LL BE RIGHT THERE!

ARTOO-DETOO, WHY DID YOU FORCE ME UP *HERE?* THE FIGHTING IS EVEN *WORSE* THAN BELOW. THERE'S NO *ESCAPE.* IT'S *MUCH* TOO HIGH FOR ME TO *JUMP.*

DRRR-PLIIT!

THERE FOLLOWS THE *KLUNK* OF A SMALLER METAL OBJECT BUMPING A SOMEWHAT *LARGER* ONE...

NOO-OOOOO!

THEN...LEIA'S DECK GUN FIRES AS LUKE ORDERED WITH SPECTACULAR RESULTS!

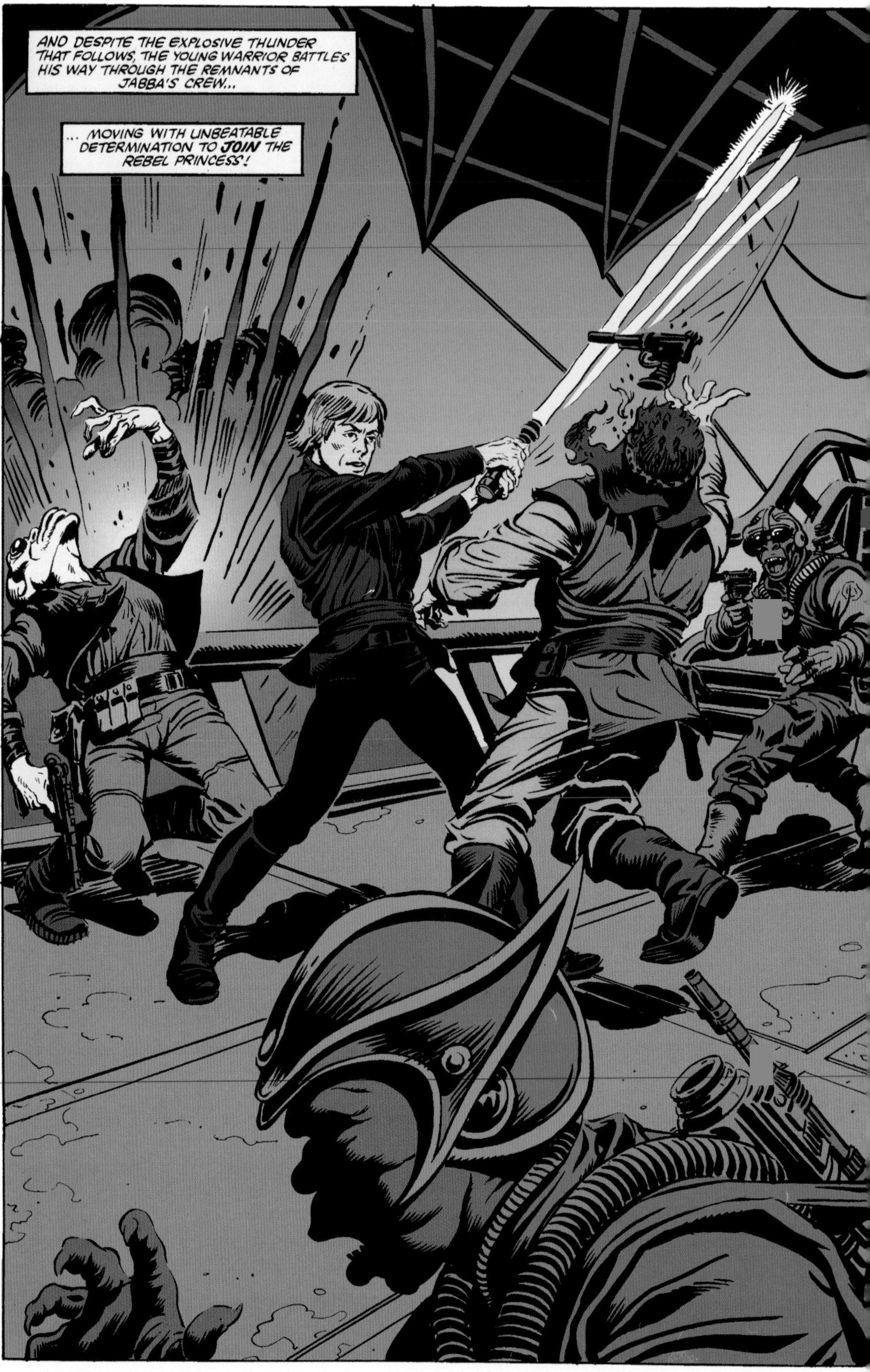
AND DESPITE THE EXPLOSIVE THUNDER THAT FOLLOWS, THE YOUNG WARRIOR BATTLES HIS WAY THROUGH THE REMNANTS OF JABBA'S CREW...
... MOVING WITH UNBEATABLE DETERMINATION TO JOIN THE REBEL PRINCESS!

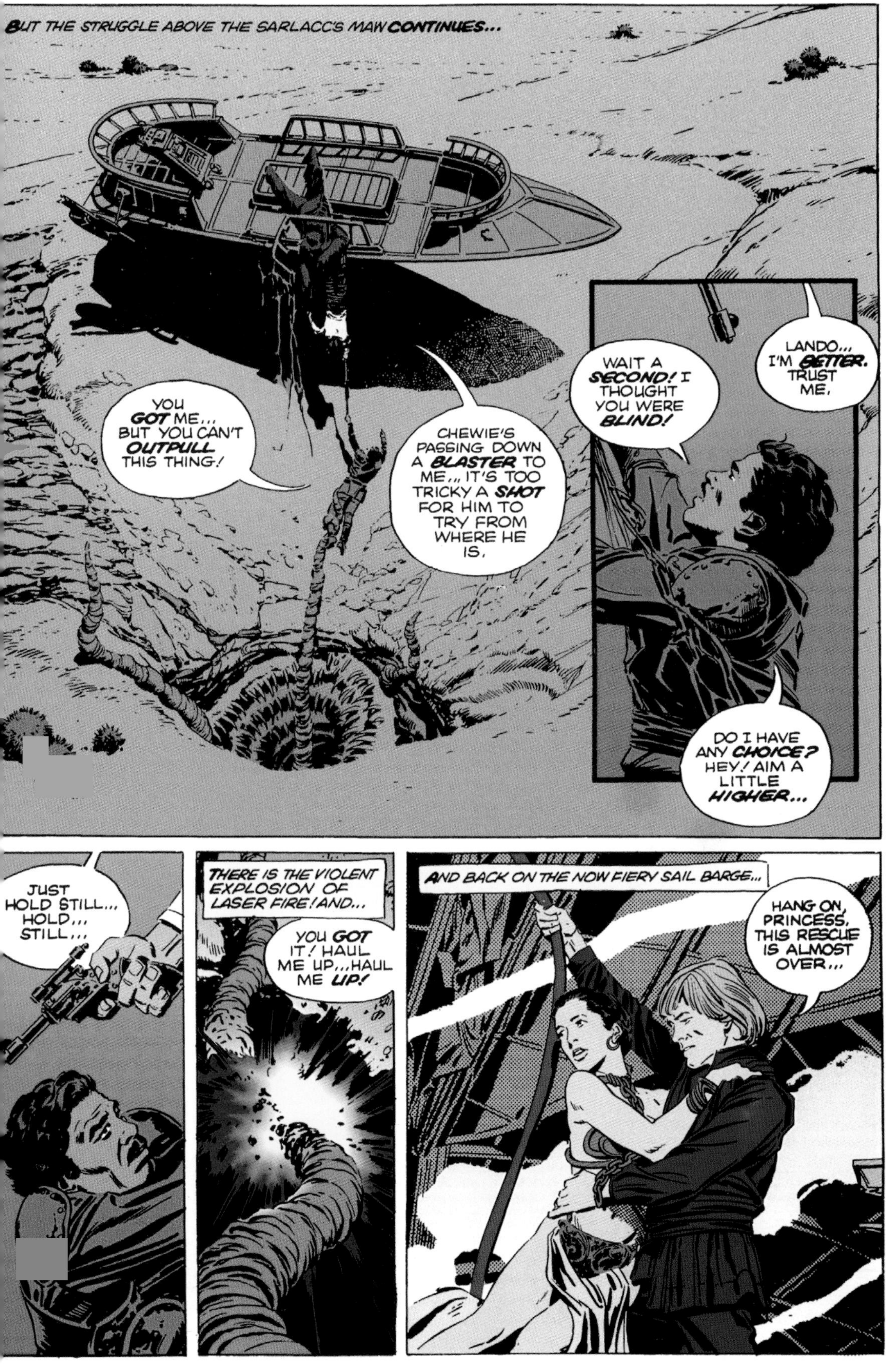
BUT THE STRUGGLE ABOVE THE SARLACC'S MAW CONTINUES...
YOU GOT ME... BUT YOU CAN'T OUTPULL THIS THING!
CHEWIE'S PASSING DOWN A BLASTER TO ME... IT'S TOO TRICKY A SHOT FOR HIM TO TRY FROM WHERE HE IS.
WAIT A SECOND! I THOUGHT YOU WERE BLIND!
LANDO... I'M BETTER. TRUST ME.
DO I HAVE ANY CHOICE? HEY! AIM A LITTLE HIGHER...
JUST HOLD STILL... HOLD... STILL...
THERE IS THE VIOLENT EXPLOSION OF LASER FIRE! AND...
YOU GOT IT! HAUL ME UP... HAUL ME UP!
AND BACK ON THE NOW FIERY SAIL BARGE...
HANG ON, PRINCESS, THIS RESCUE IS ALMOST OVER...

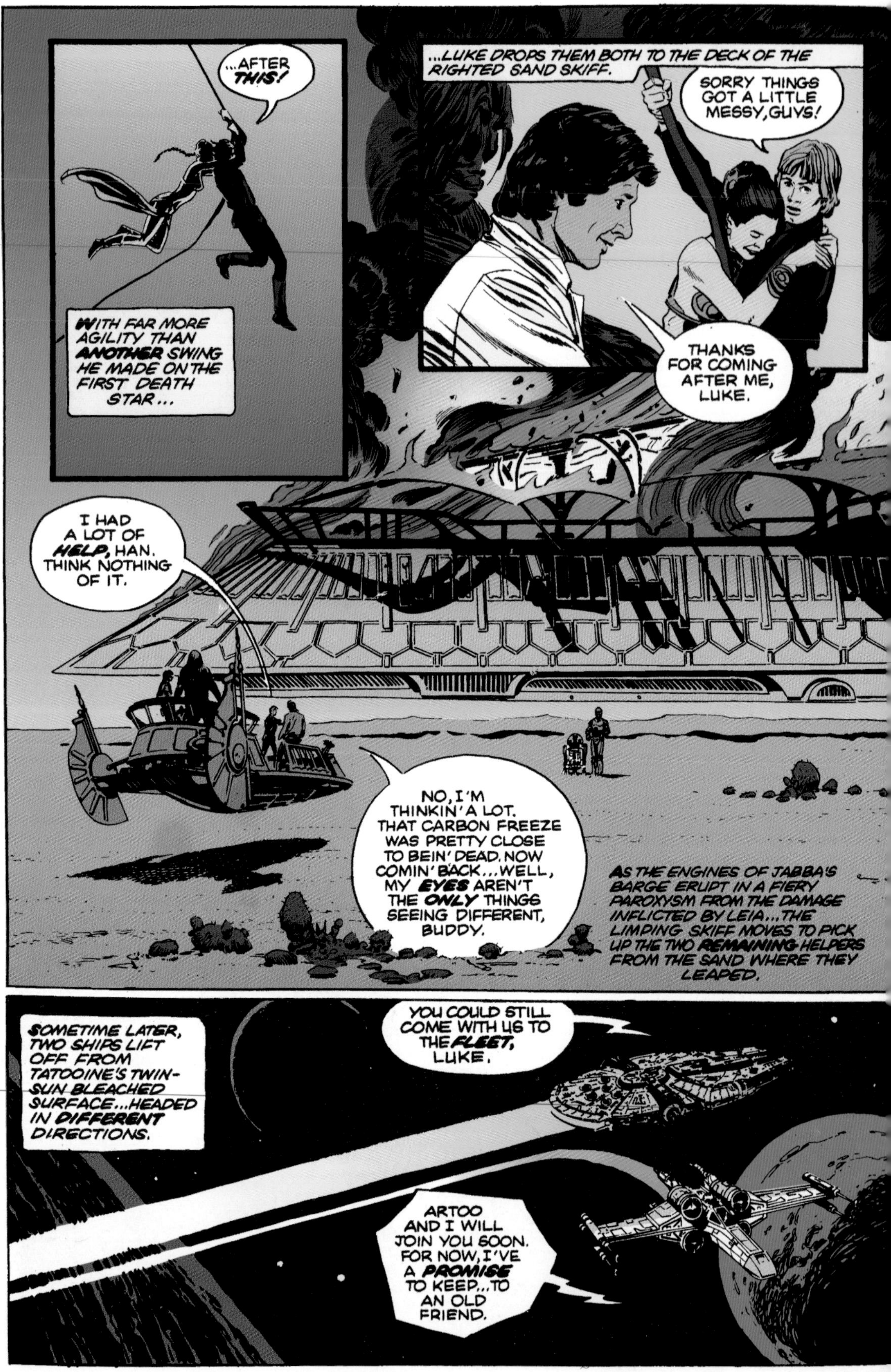
...AFTER THIS!
WITH FAR MORE AGILITY THAN ANOTHER SWING HE MADE ON THE FIRST DEATH STAR...
...LUKE DROPS THEM BOTH TO THE DECK OF THE RIGHTED SAND SKIFF.
SORRY THINGS GOT A LITTLE MESSY, GUYS!
THANKS FOR COMING AFTER ME, LUKE.
I HAD A LOT OF HELP, HAN. THINK NOTHING OF IT.
NO, I'M THINKIN' A LOT. THAT CARBON FREEZE WAS PRETTY CLOSE TO BEIN' DEAD. NOW COMIN' BACK... WELL, MY EYES AREN'T THE ONLY THINGS SEEING DIFFERENT, BUDDY.
AS THE ENGINES OF JABBA'S BARGE ERUPT IN A FIERY PAROXYSM FROM THE DAMAGE INFLICTED BY LEIA... THE LIMPING SKIFF MOVES TO PICK UP THE TWO REMAINING HELPERS FROM THE SAND WHERE THEY LEAPED.
SOMETIME LATER, TWO SHIPS LIFT OFF FROM TATOOINE'S TWIN-SUN BLEACHED SURFACE... HEADED IN DIFFERENT DIRECTIONS.
YOU COULD STILL COME WITH US TO THE FLEET, LUKE.
ARTOO AND I WILL JOIN YOU SOON. FOR NOW, I'VE A PROMISE TO KEEP... TO AN OLD FRIEND.

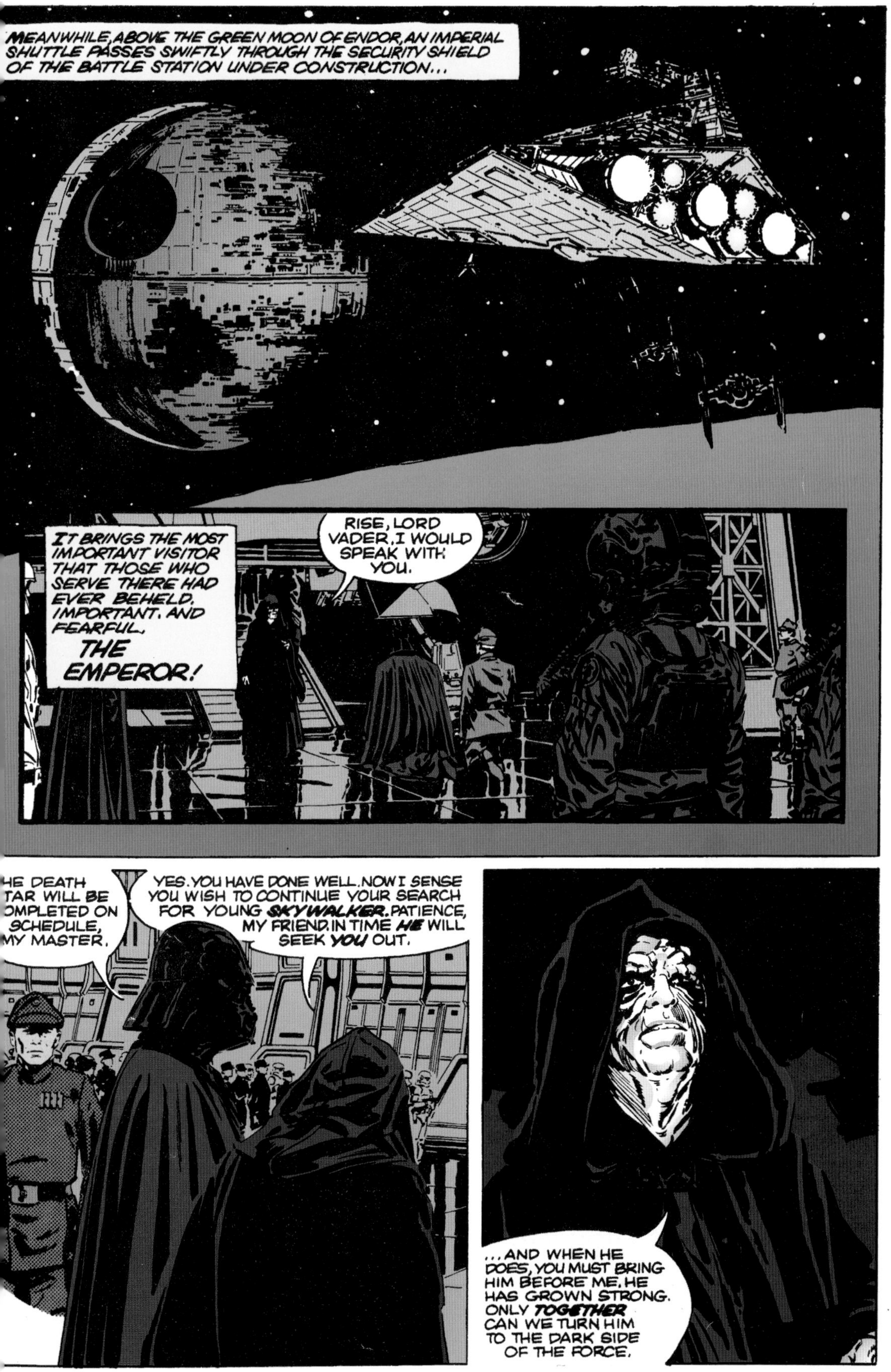
MEANWHILE, ABOVE THE GREEN MOON OF ENDOR, AN IMPERIAL SHUTTLE PASSES SWIFTLY THROUGH THE SECURITY SHIELD OF THE BATTLE STATION UNDER CONSTRUCTION...
IT BRINGS THE MOST IMPORTANT VISITOR THAT THOSE WHO SERVE THERE HAD EVER BEHELD. IMPORTANT. AND FEARFUL. THE EMPEROR!
RISE, LORD VADER. I WOULD SPEAK WITH YOU.
HE DEATH TAR WILL BE OMPLETED ON SCHEDULE, MY MASTER.
YES. YOU HAVE DONE WELL. NOW I SENSE YOU WISH TO CONTINUE YOUR SEARCH FOR YOUNG SKYWALKER. PATIENCE, MY FRIEND. IN TIME HE WILL SEEK YOU OUT.
...AND WHEN HE DOES, YOU MUST BRING HIM BEFORE ME. HE HAS GROWN STRONG. ONLY TOGETHER CAN WE TURN HIM TO THE DARK SIDE OF THE FORCE.

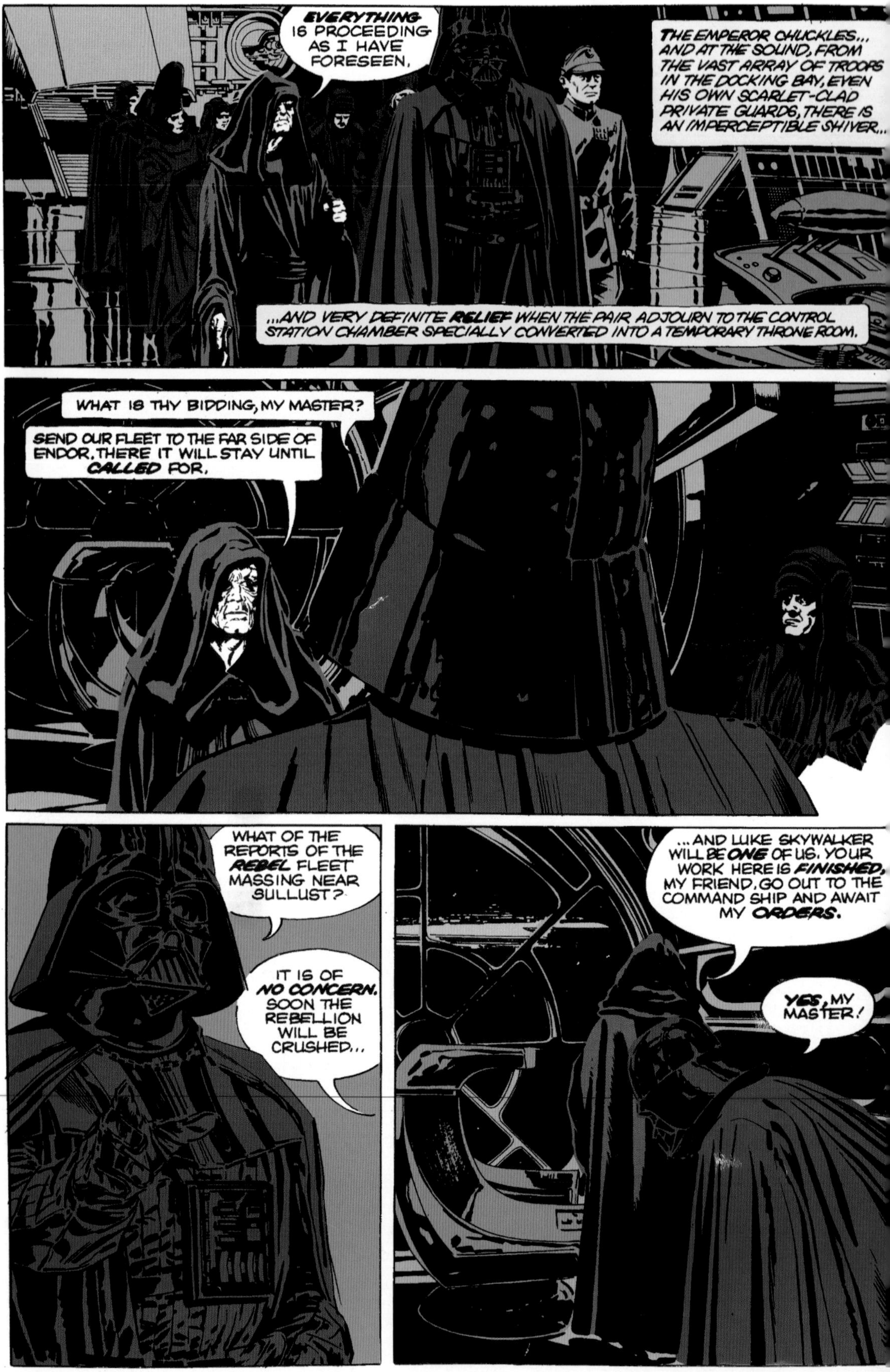
EVERYTHING IS PROCEEDING AS I HAVE FORESEEN.
THE EMPEROR CHUCKLES... AND AT THE SOUND, FROM THE VAST ARRAY OF TROOPS IN THE DOCKING BAY, EVEN HIS OWN SCARLET-CLAD PRIVATE GUARDS, THERE IS AN IMPERCEPTIBLE SHIVER...
...AND VERY DEFINITE RELIEF WHEN THE PAIR ADJOURN TO THE CONTROL STATION CHAMBER SPECIALLY CONVERTED INTO A TEMPORARY THRONE ROOM.
WHAT IS THY BIDDING, MY MASTER?
SEND OUR FLEET TO THE FAR SIDE OF ENDOR. THERE IT WILL STAY UNTIL CALLED FOR.
WHAT OF THE REPORTS OF THE REBEL FLEET MASSING NEAR SULLUST?
IT IS OF NO CONCERN. SOON THE REBELLION WILL BE CRUSHED...
...AND LUKE SKYWALKER WILL BE ONE OF US. YOUR WORK HERE IS FINISHED, MY FRIEND. GO OUT TO THE COMMAND SHIP AND AWAIT MY ORDERS.
YES, MY MASTER!

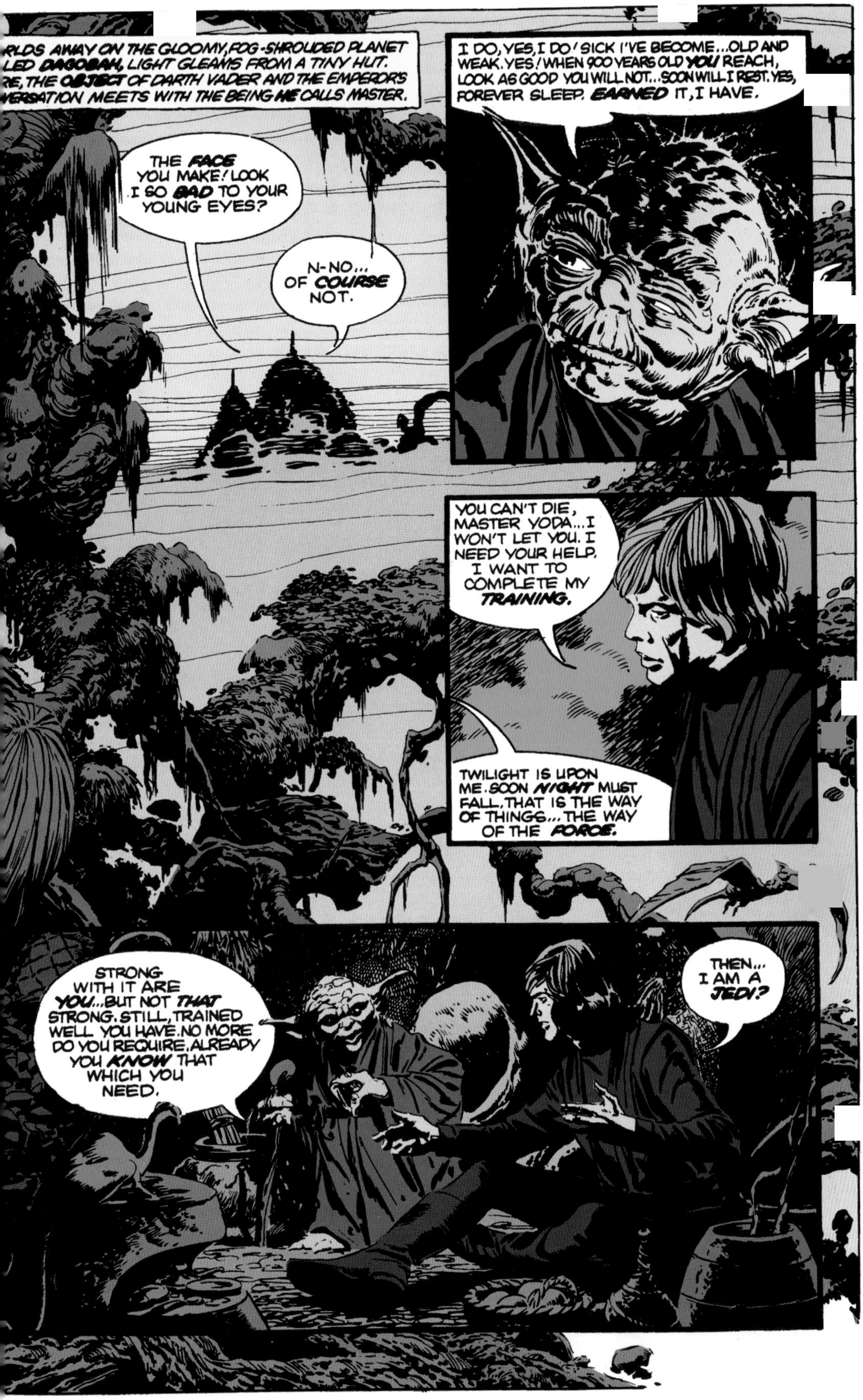
RLDS AWAY ON THE GLOOMY, FOG-SHROUDED PLANET LED DAGOBAH, LIGHT GLEAMS FROM A TINY HUT. RE, THE OBJECT OF DARTH VADER AND THE EMPEROR'S VERSATION MEETS WITH THE BEING HE CALLS MASTER.
THE FACE YOU MAKE! LOOK I SO BAD TO YOUR YOUNG EYES?
N-NO... OF COURSE NOT.
I DO, YES, I DO! SICK I'VE BECOME... OLD AND WEAK. YES! WHEN 900 YEARS OLD YOU REACH, LOOK AS GOOD YOU WILL NOT... SOON WILL I REST. YES, FOREVER SLEEP. EARNED IT, I HAVE.
YOU CAN'T DIE, MASTER YODA... I WON'T LET YOU. I NEED YOUR HELP. I WANT TO COMPLETE MY TRAINING.
TWILIGHT IS UPON ME. SOON NIGHT MUST FALL. THAT IS THE WAY OF THINGS... THE WAY OF THE FORCE.
STRONG WITH IT ARE YOU... BUT NOT THAT STRONG. STILL, TRAINED WELL YOU HAVE. NO MORE DO YOU REQUIRE. ALREADY YOU KNOW THAT WHICH YOU NEED.
THEN... I AM A JEDI?

NOT YET. ONE THING REMAINS. *VADER*... VADER YOU MUST CONFRONT. THEN, ONLY THEN, A *JEDI* YOU'LL BE.

MASTER YODA... I MUST KNOW... IS... IS DARTH VADER MY *FATHER?*

SILENCE FOLLOWS. THE LITTLE JEDI MASTER SEEMS MORE STOOPED AND EXHAUSTED THAN EVER. YET HE FEELS LUKE'S INSISTENCE, AND AT LONG LAST... ANSWERS.

TOLD YOU DID HE? YOUR FATHER HE IS, UNEXPECTED THIS IS... AND UNFORTUNATE.

THAT I KNOW THE *TRUTH...?*

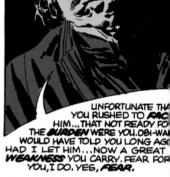

UNFORTUNATE THA' YOU RUSHED TO *FAC* HIM... THAT NOT READY FO' THE *BURDEN* WERE YOU. OBI-WAN WOULD HAVE TOLD YOU LONG AGO HAD I LET HIM... NOW A GREAT *WEAKNESS* YOU CARRY. FEAR FOR YOU, I DO, YES, *FEAR.*

MASTER YODA... I'M SORRY.

I KNOW, BUT SORRY WILL NOT HELP, LUKE... OF THE EMPEROR *BEWARE.* DO NOT UNDERESTIMATE HIS POWERS, OR SUFFER YOUR *FATHER'S* FATE YOU WILL. REMEMBER, WHEN GONE I AM,... *LAST* OF THE JEDI WILL YOU BE.

LUKE LEAVES YODA TO MUCH-NEEDED REST. BUT AS HE REJOINS A NERVOUSLY WAITING ARTOO-DETOO... HIS TEACHER'S WORDS CONTINUE TO HAUNT HIM.

I CAN'T DO IT. I CAN'T GO ON *ALONE.*

YODA AND I WILL BE WITH YOU ALWAYS.

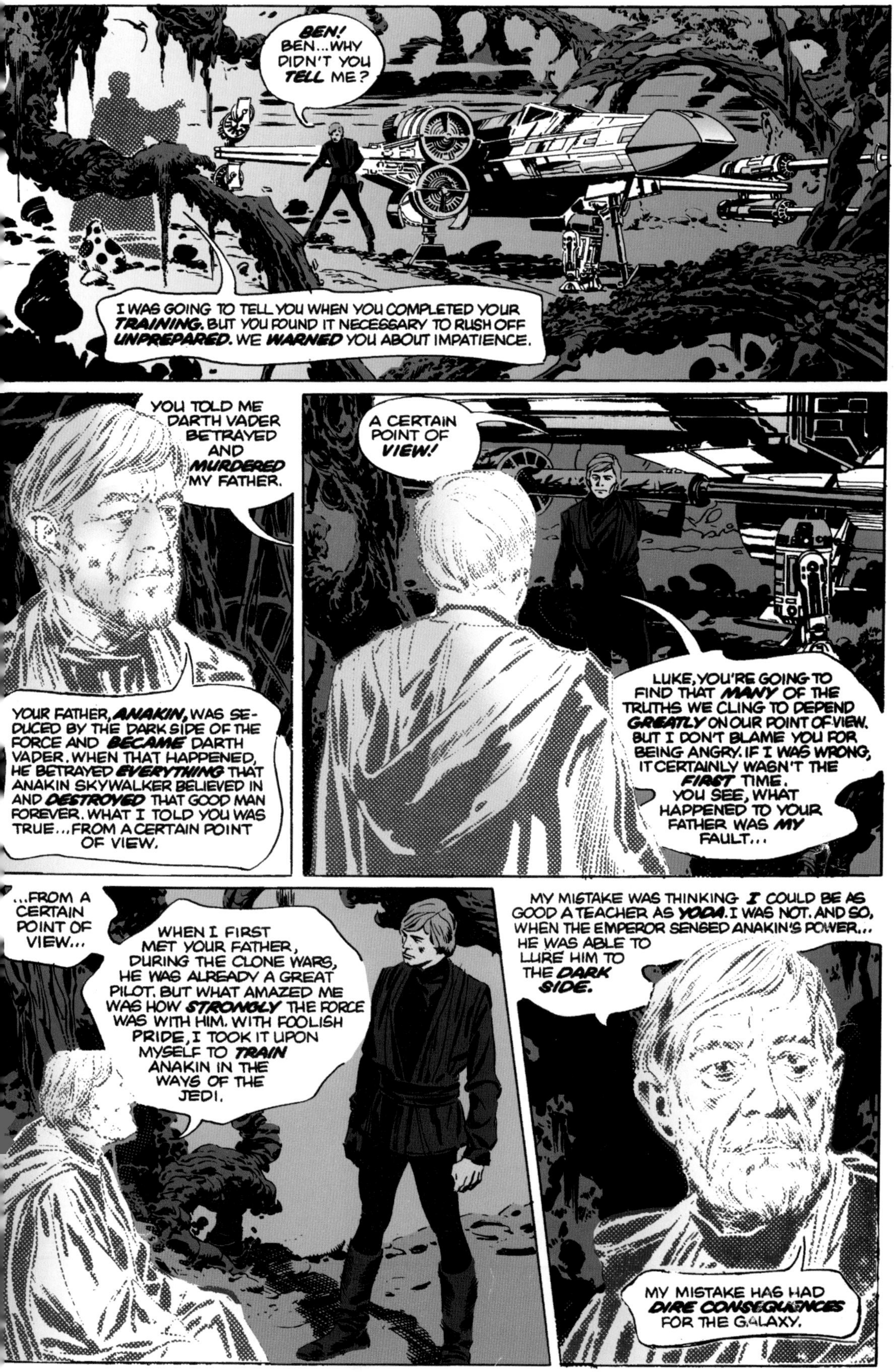
BEN! BEN...WHY DIDN'T YOU TELL ME?
I WAS GOING TO TELL YOU WHEN YOU COMPLETED YOUR TRAINING. BUT YOU FOUND IT NECESSARY TO RUSH OFF UNPREPARED. WE WARNED YOU ABOUT IMPATIENCE.
YOU TOLD ME DARTH VADER BETRAYED AND MURDERED MY FATHER.
YOUR FATHER, ANAKIN, WAS SEDUCED BY THE DARK SIDE OF THE FORCE AND BECAME DARTH VADER. WHEN THAT HAPPENED, HE BETRAYED EVERYTHING THAT ANAKIN SKYWALKER BELIEVED IN AND DESTROYED THAT GOOD MAN FOREVER. WHAT I TOLD YOU WAS TRUE...FROM A CERTAIN POINT OF VIEW.
A CERTAIN POINT OF VIEW!
LUKE, YOU'RE GOING TO FIND THAT MANY OF THE TRUTHS WE CLING TO DEPEND GREATLY ON OUR POINT OF VIEW. BUT I DON'T BLAME YOU FOR BEING ANGRY. IF I WAS WRONG, IT CERTAINLY WASN'T THE FIRST TIME. YOU SEE, WHAT HAPPENED TO YOUR FATHER WAS MY FAULT...
...FROM A CERTAIN POINT OF VIEW...
WHEN I FIRST MET YOUR FATHER, DURING THE CLONE WARS, HE WAS ALREADY A GREAT PILOT. BUT WHAT AMAZED ME WAS HOW STRONGLY THE FORCE WAS WITH HIM. WITH FOOLISH PRIDE, I TOOK IT UPON MYSELF TO TRAIN ANAKIN IN THE WAYS OF THE JEDI.
MY MISTAKE WAS THINKING I COULD BE AS GOOD A TEACHER AS YODA. I WAS NOT. AND SO, WHEN THE EMPEROR SENSED ANAKIN'S POWER... HE WAS ABLE TO LURE HIM TO THE DARK SIDE.
MY MISTAKE HAS HAD DIRE CONSEQUENCES FOR THE GALAXY.

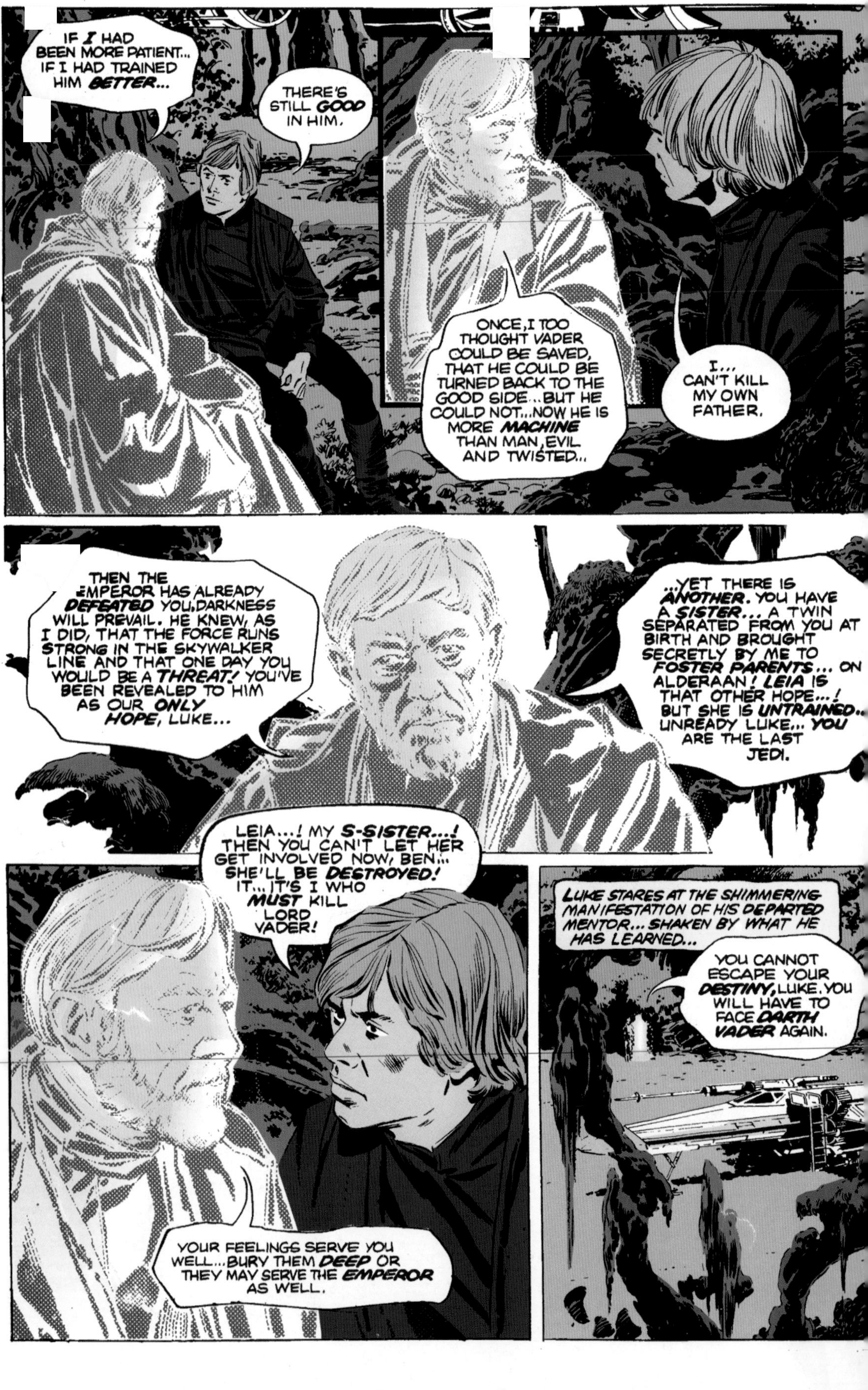
IF I HAD BEEN MORE PATIENT... IF I HAD TRAINED HIM BETTER...
THERE'S STILL GOOD IN HIM.
ONCE, I TOO THOUGHT VADER COULD BE SAVED, THAT HE COULD BE TURNED BACK TO THE GOOD SIDE...BUT HE COULD NOT...NOW HE IS MORE MACHINE THAN MAN, EVIL AND TWISTED...
I... CAN'T KILL MY OWN FATHER.
THEN THE EMPEROR HAS ALREADY DEFEATED YOU. DARKNESS WILL PREVAIL. HE KNEW, AS I DID, THAT THE FORCE RUNS STRONG IN THE SKYWALKER LINE AND THAT ONE DAY YOU WOULD BE A THREAT! YOU'VE BEEN REVEALED TO HIM AS OUR ONLY HOPE, LUKE...
...YET THERE IS ANOTHER. YOU HAVE A SISTER... A TWIN SEPARATED FROM YOU AT BIRTH AND BROUGHT SECRETLY BY ME TO FOSTER PARENTS... ON ALDERAAN! LEIA IS THAT OTHER HOPE...! BUT SHE IS UNTRAINED.. UNREADY LUKE... YOU ARE THE LAST JEDI.
LEIA...! MY S-SISTER...! THEN YOU CAN'T LET HER GET INVOLVED NOW, BEN... SHE'LL BE DESTROYED! IT... IT'S I WHO MUST KILL LORD VADER!
YOUR FEELINGS SERVE YOU WELL...BURY THEM DEEP OR THEY MAY SERVE THE EMPEROR AS WELL.
LUKE STARES AT THE SHIMMERING MANIFESTATION OF HIS DEPARTED MENTOR... SHAKEN BY WHAT HE HAS LEARNED...
YOU CANNOT ESCAPE YOUR DESTINY, LUKE. YOU WILL HAVE TO FACE DARTH VADER AGAIN.

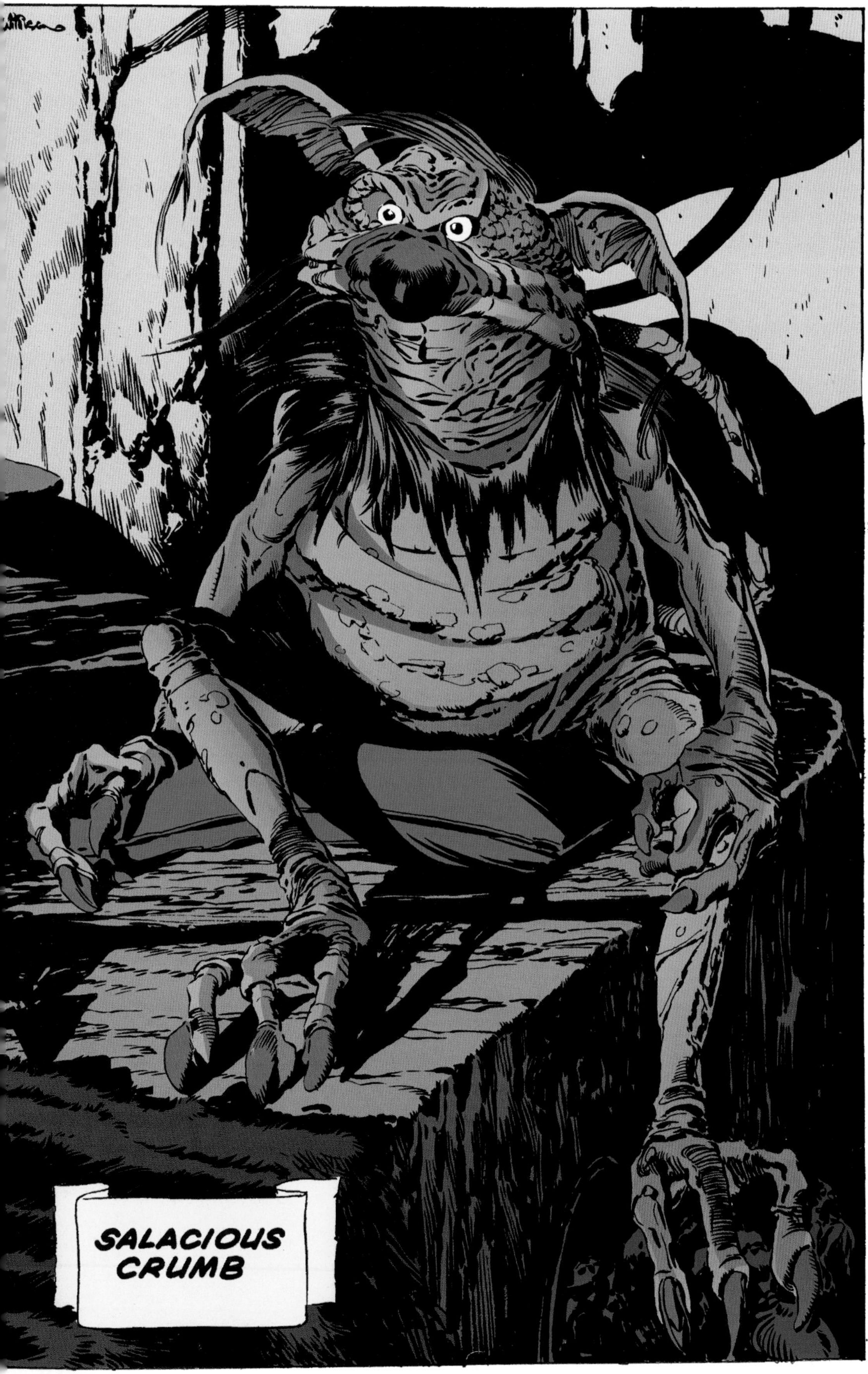
SALACIOUS CRUMB

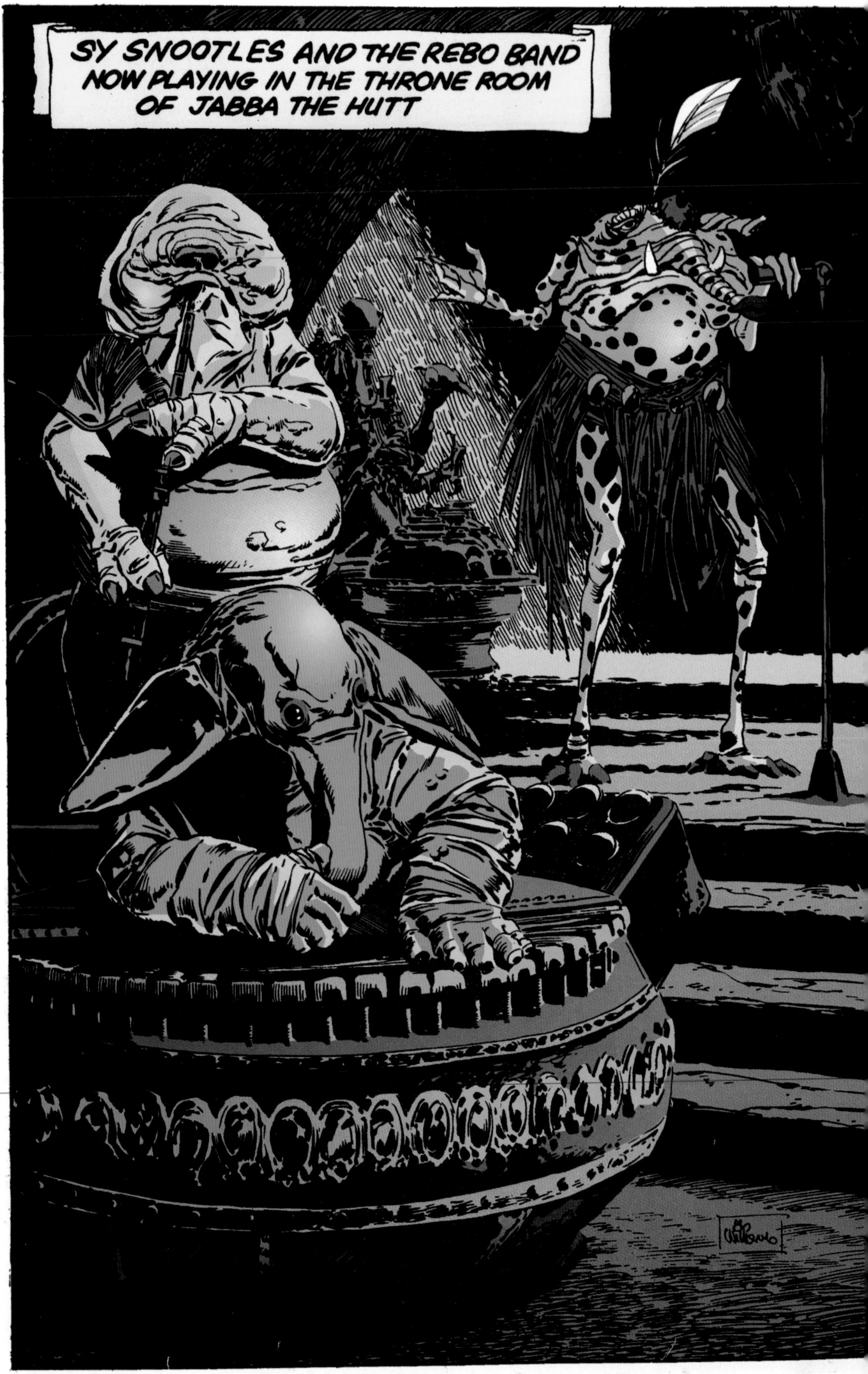
SY SNOOTLES AND THE REBO BAND
NOW PLAYING IN THE THRONE ROOM
OF JABBA THE HUTT

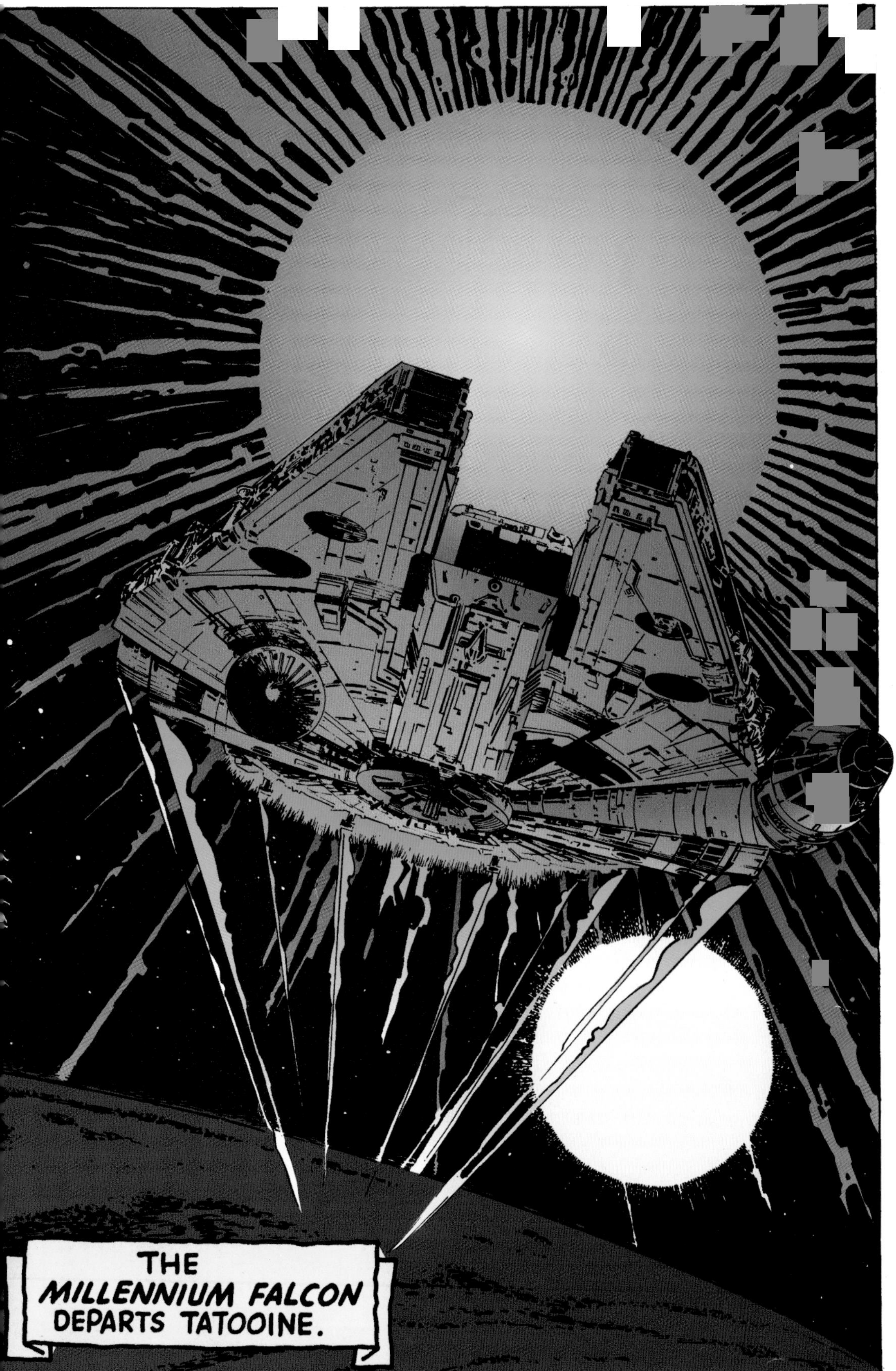
THE
MILLENNIUM FALCON
DEPARTS TATOOINE.

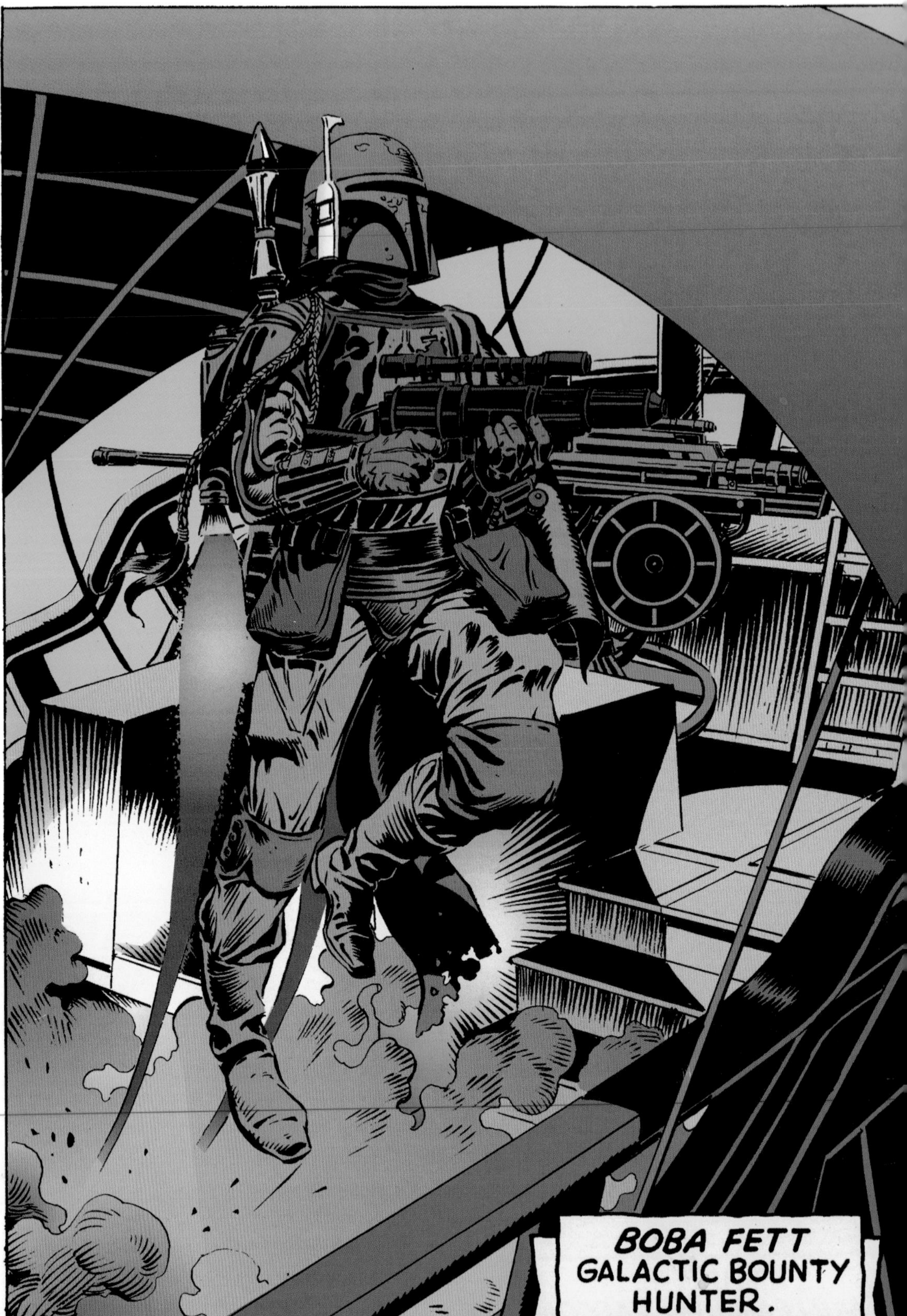
BOBA FETT
GALACTIC BOUNTY HUNTER.